To Mama, Papa, and Stephen, for your unconditional
love and support, no matter which way the wind blows.

To William—one day you'll be off on your own adventures.
Until then, I will do my best to keep you safe.

And with gratitude to anyone who takes me away
from the shallows.

About This Book

The illustrations were made using watercolor on 220gsm Daler Rowney paper with monoprinted details added to it. This book was edited by Andrea Spooner and designed by Véronique Lefèvre Sweet. The production was supervised by Nyamekye Waliyaya, and the production editor was Marisa Finkelstein. The text was set in P22 Kane, and the display type is Organika Script. The title was hand-lettered.

Sail

Dorien Brouwers

LB

Little, Brown and Company
New York Boston

We all have ships to sail
in *life*'s adventurous tale.

Yacht, tug, skiff or barge,

brig, raft, little or *large*.

Step on board and leave the shore.
Prepare yourself to *discover* more.

Raise the anchor and set the course.
Follow your *heart*. Use the wind's force.

Befriend the ocean and sail the high seas.
Ride the wild waters to go where you please.

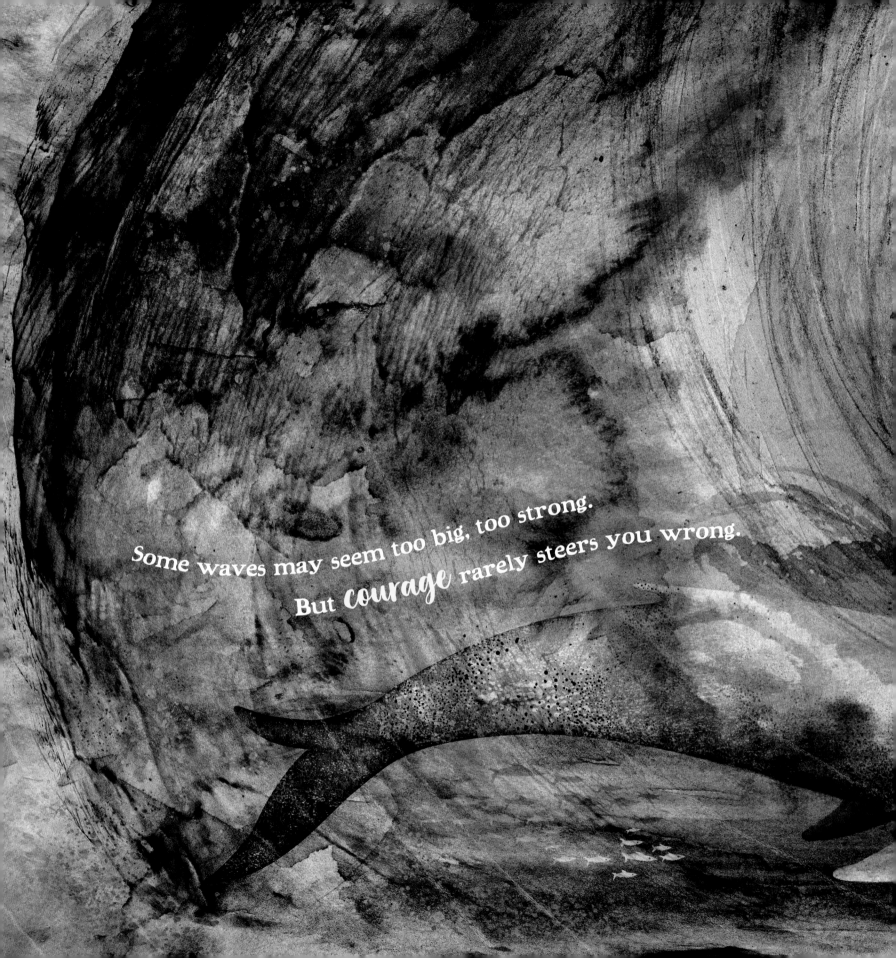

Some waves may seem too big, too strong.
But *courage* rarely steers you wrong.

When the wind refuses to blow your way,
adjust the sails without delay.

Hold on tight—the tide will turn.
Right now, there's so much more to *learn*.

And if you ever do fall in,
it's time to **try your best** to swim.

Know you're right where you need to be,
discovering *new* parts of the sea.

Search the ocean for the light.
Breathe in deep and don't lose sight.

But should your head dip right under,
open your eyes! There's a world of wonder.

Powerful wisdom is found in the deep.
Rock bottom is where you'll find TREASURE to keep.

Ride a current back to your boat.

In time, you'll find yourself *afloat.*

So cast your net wide.
Seek and you will find.
Use a compass or a star...

and you will go far.

Some Things to Think About

What are you grateful for?

Do you sometimes worry about things?

What are the most wonderful
things or most difficult things that
have ever happened to you?

What did you learn from
these experiences?

Why is it good to sometimes
face difficulty?

Who is there to help you
steer your boat?